I0720489

I'm Not One to Gossip,
So You Didn't Hear That From Me

Written By:
Jacob Grovey

Illustrated By:
Ken Mureithi

Did you see those New Zealand vacation pics Tessa posted online? I know they were fake, but that ain't no business of mine.

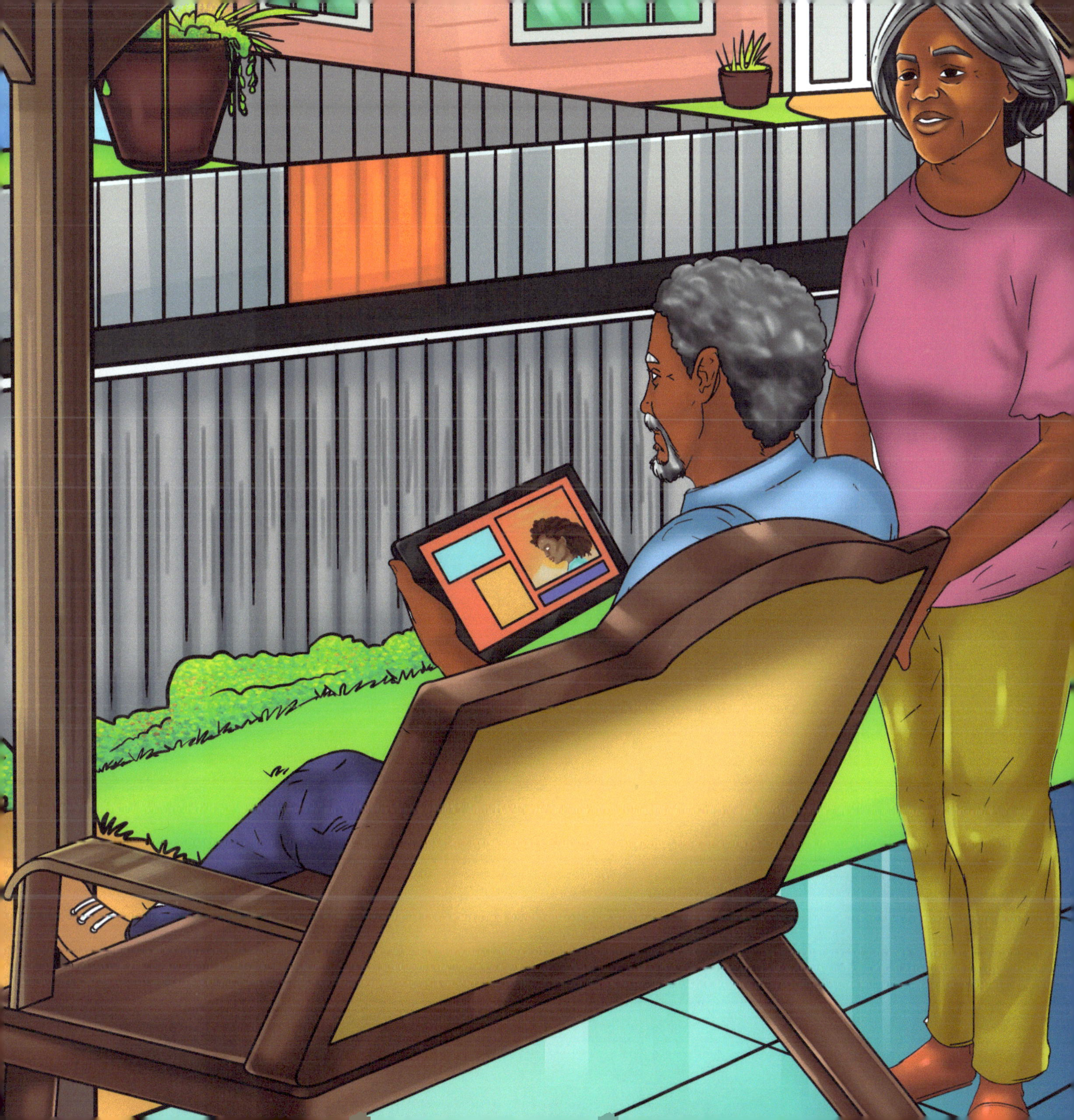

I heard Brittney talking with her friends because she thought her outfit was cute, but they said they all wished she would be quiet, they wished they could put her on mute.

Then, you have Paul, who thinks he's the best ballplayer the world has ever seen. So, how come he's never been good enough to actually make a team?

OAK
CLIFF
9

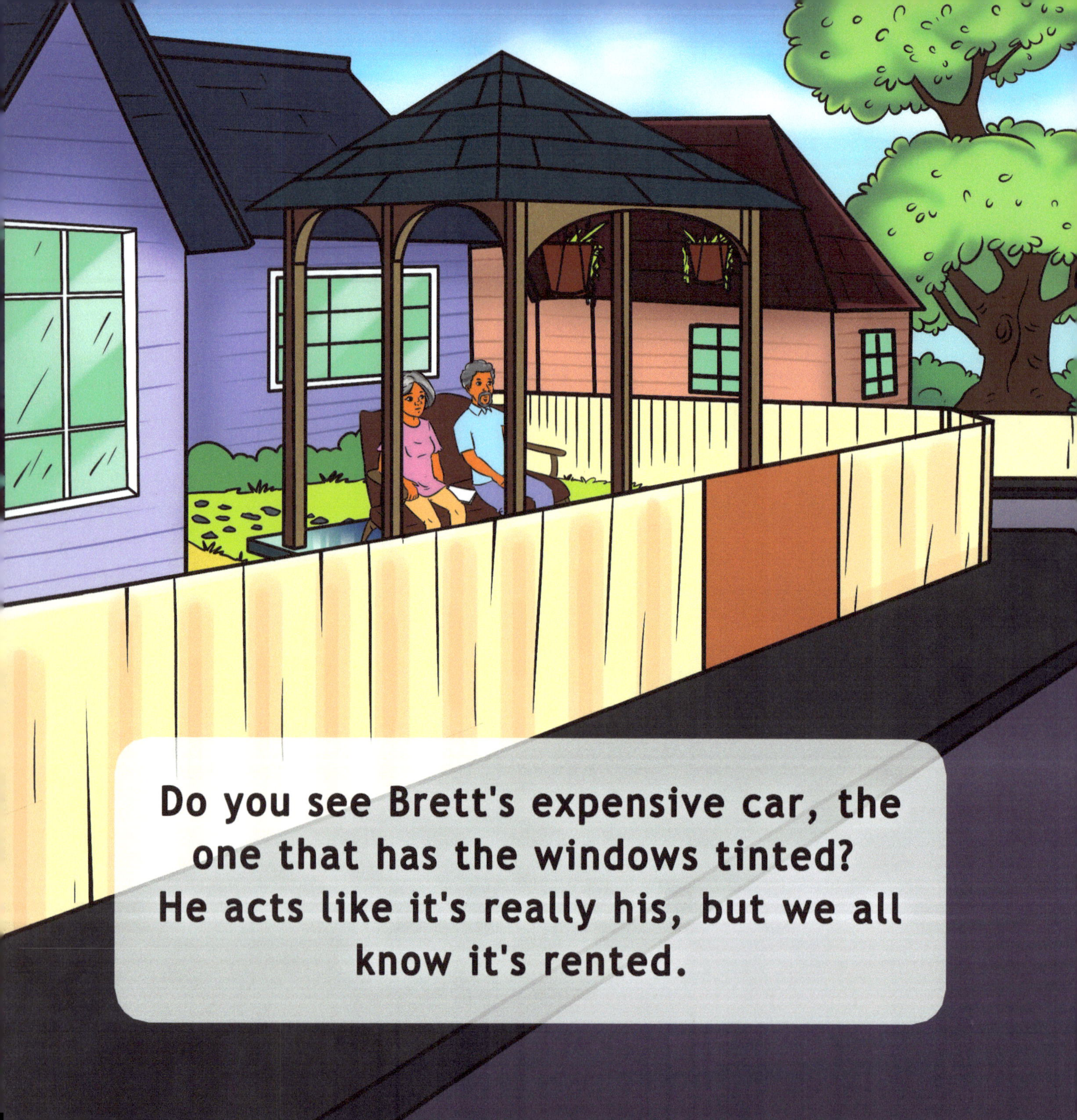

Do you see Brett's expensive car, the one that has the windows tinted? He acts like it's really his, but we all know it's rented.

RAVEN
♪

Raven keeps telling everyone she's a famous rapper, but I've never heard her songs. Who knew becoming an overnight success could take someone so long?

And her Mom ain't no better; in fact, I think she may be worse. She acts all "holier than thou" whenever we're in church.

No disrespect, but did you hear about the old couple who sits in front of their home? They relentlessly talk bad about people, and won't leave them alone.

People try to be nice to them, but they continue to be mean. Whenever they are confronted, they usually cause a scene.

They used to be popular, but now
they have no friends.
I guess when you keep gossiping, it
can cause relationships to end.

Don't talk about others behind their
back, even it's true
because if you gossip about them, then
somebody's probably gossiping about you.

I'm Not One to Gossip,
So You Didn't Hear That From Me

Written By:
Jacob Grovey

Illustrated By:
Ken Mureithi

www.ingramcontent.com/pod-product-compliance
Lightning Source LLC
Chambersburg PA
CBHW041924180726
48295CB00002B/65